The OLD MAN and the PENGUIN

A TRUE STORY of TRUE FRIENDSHIP

Written by Julie ABERY

Illustrated by Pierre PRATT

Kids Can Press

On his walk along the beach,
João hears a sorry screech.

He spies a penguin on the shore
who blinks an eye … but nothing more.

His feathers soaked in oily goo
that's black and sticky, just like glue.

Too tired to swim, too weak to stand,
he's barely moving on the sand.

João must save this little guy.
Without his help, he'll surely die.

He rubs and scrubs him.
Bubbles fly!
He cleans him off
and towels him dry.

A bowl of fish for every snack —
the penguin's strength is coming back.

They take a boat ride out to sea
to find the place he's meant to be.

João must leave him there to find
other birds of his own kind.

He's strong enough to swim away …

... but he decides he'd rather stay.

Fishy kisses, beak to nose.
Day by day, their friendship grows.

João gives him a name:
Dindim!
They snuggle close.
They play and swim.

He loves the penguin like a child,
but deep inside he knows he's wild.

Seasons change, new feathers grow.
Dindim knows it's time to go.

Instinct draws him out to sea.
A splash,

a dive,
he's swimming free.

Four months pass —
  he's back on shore,
    and waddles to
      his old friend's door.

Then João comes into sight,
and Dindim's honking with delight!

Wagging tail and dancing feet,
waiting for a sardine treat.

Time to spend eight months on land,
pampered, loved and fed by hand.

Just like clockwork every year,
João knows when he'll appear.

Pecks and strokes for happy friends,
a precious bond that never ends.

Author's Note

This is the true and remarkable story of Mr. João Pereira de Souza, a retired bricklayer, and an oil-soaked penguin.

João (sounds like Je-WOW) found the penguin while walking near his home on Proveta Beach in Rio de Janeiro, Brazil, in late spring of 2011. Exhausted and close to death, the penguin had slim chances of survival.

After cleaning and feeding him, João took him back to the sea, but his penguin friend didn't want to leave. A bond grew between them, and João named him Dindim. Every year since his first arrival, Dindim returns to Proveta Beach to spend time with his rescuer.

Dindim is a Magellanic penguin, sometimes called a banded penguin because of its unique striped pattern. Magellanic penguins are monogamous, which means they stay with the same partner for the whole of their lives. Their favorite foods are fish, such as sardines and anchovies, and squid. Magellanic penguins mostly live in South America and the Falkland Islands. In the spring, they migrate north to warmer places, such as Brazil, where Dindim was found.

All kinds of wildlife are affected yearly by oil spills in the seas and oceans. Because oil and water don't mix, spilled oil sits on the surface of the water. Any birds and mammals that swim through the slick are at risk. Animals whose fur or feathers have been covered in oil are no longer waterproof. The cold sea soaks in between the feathers, and the animals become heavy and cold. They struggle to swim and can die. It was just such an incident that brought Dindim to João's doorstep.

Spilled oil is harmful to the environment and it is also toxic to humans. Because of this, the people who help clean up the oil are highly trained. There are also wildlife professionals who rehabilitate and reintroduce animals back into their natural habitats after an oil spill. If you ever find wildlife in distress when you are out walking along the beach, contact a local wildlife rescue center.

For Sarah, Nick and Mark,
who inspired my journey — J.A.

To Senhor João Pereira de Souza — P.P.

Text © 2020 Julie Abery
Illustrations © 2020 Pierre Pratt

Kids Can Press gratefully acknowledges the financial support of the Government of Ontario, through Ontario Creates; the Ontario Arts Council; the Canada Council for the Arts; and the Government of Canada for our publishing activity.

Published in Canada and the U.S. by Kids Can Press Ltd.
25 Dockside Drive, Toronto, ON M5A 0B5

Kids Can Press is a Corus Entertainment Inc. company.

www.kidscanpress.com

The artwork in this book was rendered in pencil and digitally in Photoshop.
The text is set in Times New Roman.

Edited by Jennifer Stokes
Designed by Andrew Dupuis

Printed and bound in Shenzhen, China, in 3/2020 by C & C Offset

FSC
www.fsc.org
MIX
Paper from responsible sources
FSC® C008047

CM 20 0 9 8 7 6 5 4 3 2 1

Library and Archives Canada Cataloguing in Publication

Title: The old man and the penguin : a true story of true friendship /
written by Julie Abery ; illustrated by Pierre Pratt.

Names: Abery, Julie, author. | Pratt, Pierre, illustrator.
Identifiers: Canadiana 20190207078 | ISBN 9781525302084 (hardcover)

Subjects: LCSH: Human-animal relationships — Juvenile literature. |
LCSH: Magellanic penguin — Juvenile literature.

Classification: LCC QL696.S473 A24 2020 | DDC j598.47 — dc23